Undercover
Tailback

Undercover Tailback

•

By Matt Christopher

Illustrated by Paul Casale

SCHOLASTIC INC.
New York Toronto London Auckland Sydney

ISBN 0-590-48558-X

Text copyright © 1992 by Matthew F. Christopher. Illustrations copyright © 1992 by Paul Casale. All rights reserved. Published by Scholastic Inc., 555 Broadway, New York, NY 10012, by arrangement with Little Brown & Company. APPLE PAPERBACKS is a registered trademark of Scholastic Inc.

24 23 22 21 20 19 18 17 16 15   10 11 12 13 14 15 16/0

Printed in the U.S.A.   40

First Scholastic printing, July 1994

To Casey, Cody, and Benjamin

Undercover
Tailback

1

"P arker!"

The twelve-year-old boy crouched down and stared straight ahead. A scrawny, freckle-faced heap of helmet, pads, muddy uniform, and mean eyes glared back at him.

"Parker! You promised!" the voice from the sidelines roared again. "You said you'd take my bike to school for me! Where is it?"

Parker Nolan tried to ignore his sister's shouts and concentrate on warming up for football practice.

"Go!" he shouted.

Thud! He had made his block. Caught off balance, Freddie Ferrone hit the ground. Twisting to the left, Parker curled around the fallen lineman.

The whistle blew, signaling the start of a scrimmage. Parker reached down to help his teammate to his feet.

"Got me," said Freddie with a laugh. "Wait until next time!" He ran off to join the defensive team.

By now, Melissa Nolan was stomping across the field in a rage. "Where is it, Parker? The bus is gone now — I need my bike," shouted the angry fifth grader.

Parker took off his helmet and edged her toward the sideline. "Take it easy, Melissa." He reached over and tried to give her a hug.

"You didn't fix it, did you?" wailed the young girl. "You promised you'd ride it to school after you fixed it! I trusted you." Her brown eyes started to fill up with tears. She plopped herself down on the grass at the edge of the field.

"I *did* fix it, but then . . . it got a flat tire," Parker said, sitting down next to her. "It took so long to fix that, I was really late. Luckily, I got a ride to school at the last minute."

"You're lying, Parker. Just like always. Now I have to walk home!" Melissa turned and stomped off toward the bleachers, wiping her eyes.

The whistle blew again.

I'll play Go Fish or War with her after supper, Parker decided. That'll make it up to her.

Coach Sam Isaac didn't have a lot of patience. "You planning to practice, Nolan? Or are you so good you don't have to?"

Parker ran out to the offensive huddle at one end of the field. "What's the play?" he asked Spike Newton, the quarterback.

The blue-eyed, sandy-haired Newton just shook his head at him. Some of the other players were laughing at him. They pointed as if he were crazy.

"What's the matter?" asked Parker, confused.

Morris Comer, the burly left guard said, "Do you always play without a helmet?"

"Yeah, I ought to give you the ball right now," sneered Spike. "That'd knock some sense into you."

Parker glanced over to the sideline. He remembered taking his helmet off when he was talking to Melissa. He must have left it there. But now she was gone, and there was no helmet in sight. Where was it?

"I was just going to say something," Parker blurted out. "Someone must have stolen it. There was this creep hanging out watching us. He must have swiped it while my back was turned."

"Yeah, tell us another," snorted right tackle Darren Shultz.

"You guys never believe me," Parker protested as Mitch Crum, the all-purpose substitute offensive back, barged his way into the huddle.

"Hey, Parker, you missing something?" Mitch handed over a green-and-orange helmet with a white stripe.

6

"Where did you get my helmet? Did you find the creep who stole it?" Parker asked.

"Creep? Your sister threw it at the bench. She looked real mad," said Mitch. He turned and ran back to the sidelines.

"Hey, Parker, is it true your nose gets bigger when you tell lies, like Pinocchio?" asked Huey Walker, the chunky, red-headed center.

"Parker ought to have a real honker," snorted Cris Muldoon, the wide receiver. The whole team doubled over, choking with laughter.

"What's going on out there?" shouted Coach Isaac. "Are you guys going to play football or what?"

"Okay, guys," said Spike. "Let's see how good Parker is with his helmet on. We'll go with Thirty-two Grind."

Thirty-two Grind meant Spike would fake a quick pass, then hand the ball off to Parker. If everything went right, there would be a hole in the line just off center on the right for Parker to break through.

Parker knew that the guys wouldn't let him forget the helmet story. The best he could do now was show them that he really cared about playing ball. He hunched down and got ready for the handoff.

"Three! Two! Hut! Hut!" called Spike.

As Spike called the signals, Parker thought about Melissa's bike. So he forgot to tell her he didn't take it to school. It wasn't that long a walk home. It wasn't as though she was going to be late for something.

Suddenly he felt the ball slap against his chest. Instinctively he wrapped one arm around it and leapt forward toward the hole in the line.

But he was too late. The hole wasn't there. Recovering from their blocks, the defense had formed a solid wall. Parker came up against a mound of flailing arms and legs. Someone landed on top of him, and a whistle blew.

When they unscrambled the pileup, Parker still had the ball in his hand. He put it down and joined the huddle a few yards away.

"Still got your helmet, Parker?" joked Cris.

"Okay, guys, let's get off Parker's case and play some ball," grumbled Moose Brogan, the tight end. "I want to catch some passes."

"Me, too," said Stacy Fishburne, the other wide receiver. "How about Seventeen Red?"

Spike nodded, and they lined up for the next play. All Parker had to do was block his man. That would help give Spike time to throw.

It worked. Stacy took an easy fifteen-yard pass and ran it offside for a gain of twenty.

"Nice pass," called Coach Isaac. "Okay, let's mix them up. I want to see some running, too. And you linemen, how's about opening a few holes for the runners?"

But Spike tried another pass, this time to Moose. He hit for a gain of ten yards.

His next pass, to Cris Muldoon, was right on the mark, too.

"Okay, Spike," called Coach Isaac. "Let's see some running plays."

Crouched down in the huddle, Fabian deRosa, the rugged fullback, muttered, "Give me the ball. I'll show him some running."

"Naw, that's what they're expecting," said Spike. "Let's try Thirty-two Grind again."

Putting me on the spot, thought Parker. Okay, why not?

They lined up, and Huey snapped the ball to Spike. The fake pass was followed by the hand-off. This time the hole was right where it was supposed to be. Parker sped through it into the open field.

If this were a real game, I'd see some points on the scoreboard, he thought as he trotted across the goal line.

Excited but a little tired when he came off the field, Parker sat down on the bench. Coach Isaac was standing a few yards away, talking to Rook Stubbs, the trainer. Parker could just make out the coach's words.

"That Parker," said the coach, nodding over his shoulder toward the bench. "Sometimes, you just have to hand it to him." He quickly added, "I mean the football."

The rest of the scrimmage went pretty well. Parker made a few more good plays and had some nice runs. When he concentrated on what he was doing, he was a strong offensive runner.

On the way to the locker room, a few players stopped at the drinking fountain.

Mitch asked Parker, "What was with your little sister, anyhow?"

"Who knows?" Parker shrugged. "Kids!"

"Sisters!" said Moose.

"Girls!" said Cris.

Everyone laughed.

Parker quickly showered and got into his school clothes. Then he took his pads and dirty practice uniform to the equipment room around the corner.

"Where's your helmet?" asked Rook Stubbs. In addition to his job as trainer, Stubbs took care of just about everything else — except coaching.

Parker blinked. "I guess I left it near my locker. Wait a minute — I'll go get it."

Stubbs shook his head. "Take a break, Parker. I have it right here."

"Where'd you get it? Somebody must have tried to steal it again," Parker stammered.

"Could've," said Stubbs. "Or it could be that you left it near the fountain outside. A couple of the guys gave Coach Isaac some lip. He sent them back to do a few laps while you were getting cleaned up. One of them brought it in."

The door next to the equipment room had opened. Coach Isaac had come out and had heard Stubbs's story.

"You seem to be having some memory problems, Parker," Coach Isaac said. "I know just the thing for it. Get to practice early tomorrow and do fifteen laps. And don't give me a short count. I may not be there to watch you, but I'll know."

Parker didn't say a word. He just nodded and picked up his gym bag. Fifteen laps! On top of his regular warmups? By the time scrimmage starts, I'll need a stretcher, he thought ruefully.

2

"How was school today?" asked Mrs. Nolan after dinner. "You've both been very quiet. Anything wrong?"

Parker watched to see if Melissa would squawk about her bike. But the ten-year-old girl was silent.

"Nothin' special, Mom," he said. "Just the usual. Classes. Football practice."

"You didn't get hurt during practice, Parker, did you?"

She always worried about him. He used to talk about football with his father all the time. But in the three years since Mr. Nolan had died, Parker had shrugged off any discussion about the game.

"No, I'm fine, really," he said. "C'mon, Melissa, I'll play cards with you."

"That should really make me wonder if something's wrong." Mrs. Nolan laughed. "But I'm not going to worry about it. This working gal is going to soak in a nice hot tub for a while. Then I'm going to bed. Don't stay up too late — and no watching those horror movies on TV."

"They're not horror movies," protested Melissa. "They're called whodummits."

"Who*dunits*," Parker said.

"I don't know," replied Melissa innocently.

Mrs. Nolan rolled her eyes and went upstairs.

She'd hardly left the room before Melissa had dealt out the whole deck of cards.

The game of War began.

Parker stared down at the pile of cards in front of him. He turned one over. It was a nine.

Slowly Melissa turned over a card: a ten.

She scooped up both overturned cards and tucked them under her pile.

Parker stretched and turned over another card. It was the ace of clubs.

Melissa turned over hers: the ace of diamonds.

"War!" she shouted, her voice filled with joy.

A few minutes later, she wasn't so happy. Parker had collected the pile of cards and was now ahead. Several hands later, his stack was even thicker.

"Listen, Melissa," he said. "Let's take a break for a minute, okay? Why don't you watch some TV or something?"

"What's the matter, Parker?" she asked. " 'Fraid I'm going to stage a comeback?"

"Naw," he replied, "I'm really just not in the mood for War right now. I've got other things on my mind."

"Like what?" she asked him seriously.

Should I tell her? he wondered. It's not that big a deal. But what did he have to lose?

"Well, practice was kind of rough today," he began. "Everyone was on my case over my stupid helmet."

He told her about getting razzed by the guys for leaving it on the sidelines. That wasn't too bad, he pointed out. But then he described what

15

happened at the equipment room and the coach's reaction. He didn't mind having to do the extra laps, he confessed. It was the coach's attitude that hurt.

"And that's the whole story?" she asked.

"That's it."

"Everything?"

"What is this, the third degree?"

Melissa swept the cards up from the table and began to put them in their box.

"I don't know why you're so surprised the coach didn't believe you. You know, Parker, you're not exactly famous for telling the truth," she said in her smug, ten-year-old, matter-of-fact voice. Just the sound of it bugged him.

"Oh, sure, you know everything, and you always tell the truth, the whole truth, and nothing but the truth," he said.

Melissa shrugged.

"I know I'm not the one making up stories," she said.

"Like what?"

"Like telling everyone that Dad played football for the Florida Gators," she answered. "Dad didn't go to college, and you know it. You just picked that team 'cause you like slimy things like lizards and alligators."

"So what?" he said. "Dad could've been an All-Star if he went to a college with a great team like the Gators. It was just his rotten luck that he had to go to work right after high school."

"And what about saying that Mom went to college to become a lawyer? Sure, she was studying law. But she had to give it up after two years on account of you."

"Me?"

"You know what I mean . . . you being born."

"Yeah, but she probably would have gone back if you didn't turn up, too!"

"Thanks a lot, Parker," she said. "You know that's not true. If Mom really wanted to go back to school, she could have after Dad died. And who knows, maybe someday she will be a lawyer — if she wants to, and not because you made up some story."

Melissa had been just seven when Mr. Nolan

died of leukemia. Parker had never really known how she felt about losing her father. He only knew how sad and lonely it made him feel when he thought about it. In his own way, he had tried to fill in for his father with Melissa. But it was hard sometimes — especially when his kid sister was so smart.

Still, he was a little surprised that she hadn't mentioned the bicycle incident. It wasn't like her to give up a chance to make him squirm. Was she finally growing up?

Maybe Joni would know. Joni Anderson was his best friend, and she knew Melissa pretty well, too.

The following day, Parker sat down next to Joni in the cafeteria. They had finished their tuna melts and were nibbling on potato chip crumbs when Joni brought up his favorite subject: reptiles.

"We just got to the chapter on reptiles in our science book," she said. "I wish I felt the way you do about them."

"Newts . . . lizards . . . even iguanas," he said. "I love 'em all."

"Even dinosaurs?" Joni said.

"Yep." Parker smiled. "Love the big guys, too. Even the medium ones. 'Specially those. Love those Gators!"

Joni laughed. "Are you still talking about reptiles now, or have we switched to football?"

Parker's dad had been a big fan of the Gators, a college football team. Parker's smile faded when he remembered the fun they used to have watching games together.

He quickly recovered. "Guess I just love them both."

"Okay," said Joni. "We'll have gatorburgers for lunch tomorrow."

Just then, the two wide receivers, Stacy and Cris, walked by, lunch trays in hand.

"Hey, isn't that Parker Nolan, the famous tailback without a helmet?" asked Cris.

"I don't know," answered Stacy. "Let's see if he has number thirty shaved on the back of his head!"

They broke themselves up laughing as they swaggered by.

"What was that all about?" asked Joni.

"Just a couple of wise guys," mumbled Parker. "Dumb joke. Doesn't mean anything."

"Parker!" she insisted. "It has to mean *something*."

"Oh . . . I . . . uh . . . misplaced my helmet a couple of times. And I really thought it got stolen. But they didn't believe me."

"Why not? Things get taken all the time," she said.

"Oh, they have this thing. They think I make up stories all the time."

"What? Who do they think they are, the Supreme Court?" she fumed. "I'd like to tell them a thing —"

"Take it easy, Joni," Parker said. "Things like that don't bother me. Here, I'll take your tray back. Just put it on top of mine."

Parker seemed cool as a cucumber, but he was annoyed. It seemed like someone was always on his case about something. He frowned when he remembered the extra laps he had to run before practice that afternoon. The two trays he was carrying suddenly seemed a lot heavier.

3

Parker's good spirits had returned by that
afternoon. The minute his last class was
over, he headed for the locker room. After being chewed out the day before, he was deter-
mined to show Coach Isaac what he was really
made of.

He was very early. The equipment room was
closed, and the window in the door to the coach's
office was dark. Coach Isaac wasn't there yet.

But the locker room was open. Parker went
in, dumped his books in his locker, and got un-
dressed. He put on a gray T-shirt and matching
sweatpants. They had a dark green *K* for Kudzus
on them. He tugged a gray hooded sweatshirt
on top.

He started to do a few torso twists and knee bends. Then he heard voices outside the locker room.

I guess some of the guys are out there, he thought. They'll probably give me a razzing for getting in trouble with the coach.

But whose voices are those, anyhow? he wondered. Is that Mitch? Moose? Through the wall, it was hard to tell. It could even have been a bunch of girls heading for gymnastics practice.

But when he stepped outside the locker room, there was no one in sight. Whoever had been there was gone. Then all of a sudden, someone wearing a gray hooded sweatsuit ducked out of the coach's office — and quickly bolted around the corner. It happened so fast, he couldn't tell who it was. But he did notice one odd thing: whoever it was had a small point-and-shoot camera swinging from one hand.

Parker frowned. Why would someone be in Coach's office with a camera? Suspicious, Parker took off after the stranger. But it was too late. The corridor led to the back exit from the school.

It was already filled with kids milling about on their way home. There was no way to pick out anyone in that crowd.

He went back toward the coach's office. The window was still dark, but the door was slightly ajar.

Parker pushed the door open, and the light from the hallway spilled into the office.

"Coach? Coach Isaac?" he called softly.

What did he think he was going to find — a dead body behind the desk? Was that why he was whispering?

What a dope! he thought.

There was no body behind the desk. There was nothing unusual at all in the office.

Coach Isaac was one of those neat types, he noticed. Except for the big loose-leaf Kudzu playbook, his desk was clean and uncluttered.

The master playbook was so fat with all the plays the coach had used over the years that it was hard to keep it lying flat. The plays were carefully drawn in dark marker, each on a separate page wrapped in a cellophane protector.

25

A green metal paperweight was holding down one side of the open book.

Parker picked up the paperweight.

It was an alligator! In fact, it was a lot like a model he'd brought in to show his General Science class when they were studying reptiles.

I wonder if Coach Isaac is a Gators fan, Parker thought. Hey, when he finds out they're my favorite team, maybe I'll score some extra points with him.

Then he came to his senses. The only way I'm going to score any points, he thought, is by getting my butt out there and doing those laps.

Parker was about to put the gator back on the open playbook when the overhead light went on. He hadn't even heard anyone come in.

"What are you doing here, Parker?" demanded Coach Isaac. "And what are you doing with that?" He pointed at the paperweight, still in Parker's hand.

"It was really weird, Coach," said Parker. "I just saw someone go flying out of here. But the

26

light wasn't on. So I thought something might be funny. I came in here to check."

Coach Isaac shook his head. "You really do have a million stories, don't you!"

"Honest, Coach Isaac," said Parker. "This guy just came tearing out of here a few minutes ago. He was wearing a gray sweatshirt like mine, and he had a little camera."

"Yeah, yeah," said Coach Isaac. "Tell me another. I suppose he was the one who took the master playbook off the shelf and left it opened up on my desk. Of course, you wouldn't do that, would you?"

" 'Course not," said Parker. "Why should I?"

"Maybe you wrote your moves down wrong in your own playbook," the coach suggested, "and decided to take a peek at mine to double-check them. Or maybe you're going to tell me your book was stolen?"

"Mine's in my locker, right now," insisted Parker. "I could go and get it for you. . . ."

"Never mind." Coach Isaac sighed. "Parker, what are you doing with my paperweight?"

"I . . . I found it on top of the playbook," said Parker. It didn't seem like the right time to mention his interest in the Gators.

"Well, that's not where it was when I left this office, I can tell you that," stormed the coach. "Now, just put it down and get going. I don't want to see you in this office again unless I tell you to cross that threshold. Get that?"

"Yes, Coach," said Parker. He placed the green gator down on the desk with care.

"And what about those laps?" the coach asked. "Think I forgot?"

Parker wasn't sure, but he thought he caught a small smile at the edges of the coach's mouth.

"No, siree!" said Parker. "I'm on my way."

He finished his laps just in time to join that afternoon's practice.

It didn't go well for the offense. The defense was too familiar with their plays.

When the runners started fumbling and passes were getting intercepted regularly, Coach Isaac blew the whistle.

He gathered the offense over to one side of the field while the defense took a break.

"I don't know what's the matter," grumbled Spike. "What are we doing wrong?"

"Not a whole lot," said Coach Isaac. "You're running the plays the way I drew them up. But you have to remember, these guys are used to the way we operate."

"What do you mean?" asked Fabian.

"There's a routine," said the coach. "They've come to expect that you're going to do certain things the same way every time."

"You mean we have to mix it up more?" asked Parker.

"That's it," said the coach.

"But we only have so many plays," said Fabian. "We can't just make up new ones on the spot."

"Yeah, we have to stick to our plays," insisted Cris. "I mean, that's all we know."

"I'm not telling you to abandon the plays I've taught you," explained the coach. "You just have to learn to surprise the opposition. For instance, when was the last time you ran the same play twice in a row?"

His question was answered by shrugs and vacant stares.

"Okay, here's a little trick you ought to learn right now," he went on. "When you want to repeat a play right away, all you do is call the signal backwards."

"Hey, that's neat!" said Moose. "That'll confuse 'em."

"You can use that when you're running out of time," said the coach. "Or you can linger as long as possible in the huddle so that they'll be watching for some complicated new play."

"And then, bam, you hit them with the one you just ran," said Huey. "Not bad!"

They lined up for some more practice. The defense was still hitting hard. Spike called a draw play that produced a ten-yard loss with Parker at the bottom of a big pileup.

"That's a good play," Spike announced in the

huddle. "We should have picked up some yard-age. Let's go with it again."

At the line, he barked out the signals — backward, the way the coach had said.

As soon as the play began, Parker could tell the defense was unprepared for what was happening.

This time, as soon as the ball hit his hands, he broke away and carried it into the clear beyond any defenseman's reach.

It was his happiest moment of the day.

That evening, the scene in the coach's office kept coming back to Parker. He was sure the stranger in the gray sweatshirt had been carrying a camera, but what had he been doing in Coach Isaac's office with all the lights off? Parker tried to study his math, but he ended up doing more doodling than calculating.

He couldn't sit still. Melissa had finished her homework and was looking at a magazine.

Parker sighed and picked up the deck of cards. "Come on, let's play another game of War."

"No, I don't feel like it," said Melissa.

"Want to watch TV?" he asked.

"There's nothing on," she said, staring at the magazine.

"You still mad?" he said. "About the bike?"

"No," she replied.

"Yes, you are."

"No, I'm not!"

"What are you mad about?" he asked.

"Nothing, nothing, nothing!" she insisted. "What's bothering you, anyhow?"

"Why should I tell you? You'll just tell me I'm making things up, like everyone else," he said.

"I'm your sister, Parker," she said. "*I* can tell the difference. Besides . . ."

"Besides what?"

"Besides, if you're really in trouble, you know I'm on your side."

"It's not like that," he explained. "Well, here's what happened *today*."

He began his story with the mysterious person

in the sweatshirt and ended it in the coach's office.

"So, what do *you* think, Parker?" she asked.

He got up and stretched. Then he put his arms behind his head and twisted back and forth. Then he did a few toe touches.

"Why do you always wiggle around like that when you're thinking?" she asked. "Just stand still and tell me your theory."

"I think there was something really fishy going on," he announced.

"Fishy? What do you mean?"

"This is going to sound kind of crazy, but . . . well" — he hesitated — "maybe that guy who ran off with the camera was taking pictures."

"That's usually what people do with a camera, Parker," Melissa said sarcastically.

"Don't get wise," he said. "I mean, I think he was taking pictures of the coach's playbook. And he was using the paperweight to hold it in place."

"That's pretty far out," said Melissa. "Why would anyone want to do that?"

"Maybe one of the guys on the team wanted

a copy to study," Parker suggested. "Or maybe it was a scout from one of the pro teams who wanted the inside track —"

"There you go, Parker, making up stories," Melissa said. "That's how you start to get into trouble. No wonder the coach didn't believe you. Nobody does. You're always telling lies, one after the other."

"I wasn't lying," Parker insisted. "I'd never lie about something really important."

"Hah!" snorted Melissa. "That's the biggest lie of all!"

4

S aturday morning dawned sunny and cold.
By ten o'clock it had warmed up, but there
was still a trace of dew on the grassy gridiron.

At one end of the field, the Lawrence Leopards were going through their drills. Their white
uniforms with blue trim and red numbers looked
bright and flashy.

The Kensington Kudzus, in their orange uniforms with white numbers, were just about
through with their warmup when the first
whistle blew. The referee signaled that it was
time to start the game.

Nick Watson, the Leopards' quarterback, met
up with Spike Newton for the Kudzus at the
center of the field.

The Leopards won the coin toss. They elected to receive and ran off to the east end of the field to get ready.

"Okay, guys, this is it," said Spike. Besides having a strong throwing arm, the Kudzus' quarterback was the team's best placekicker.

The Kudzus lined up for their attack downfield.

Spike kicked the ball high but not very far. It dropped into the hands of a receiver on the Leopards' thirty-five yard line. But the runner didn't get anywhere. Tackle Billy Wilson brought him down just shy of the forty.

Seated on the bench, the Kudzus' offense tried to guess what the Leopards would do with the ball.

"They're in pretty good field position," offered Huey. "I bet they run the ball."

"Nah, first and ten on their own forty?" said the Kudzu tackle Tru Ballinger. "They'll figure our guys are gonna guess that. Watch for the pass — the long bomb."

He was right about the pass but wrong about

the distance. Watson threw a short screen pass. His tight end grabbed it with no trouble. But Jerry Lawrence, the Kudzus' cornerback, was on him in a flash and made the tackle.

It was a gain of four yards. Second and six to go for a first down.

This time Watson called a running play. He handed off the ball to his fullback, Rick Fanelli, who broke through the Kudzus' line. He crossed the midfield stripe and was heading for daylight. But a horde of orange uniforms drove him off-side at the Kudzus' twenty yard line.

"C'mon, you guys," called Coach Isaac from the sideline. "Dig in!"

The Kudzus' defense did the best they could. But the Leopards kept inching their way forward with a series of short running plays.

"They're too smart to put the ball in the air this close," said Spike. "Too much to lose."

At a signal from Coach Isaac, the Kudzus' defense called a time-out and came over to the sidelines.

As the whole team crowded around, he

pointed out some of the mistakes that they were making.

Terry Gold, the Kudzus' right guard, spoke up.

"I noticed something, too," he said. "If Watson looks to the right before he starts to call signals, it usually means he's going to pass. That'll give us a shot at him."

"You've been watching too much football on TV," said Bucky Burke, the nose tackle.

"Just keep your eyes open and play some heads-up ball," said the coach. "Terry could be right."

He was. On the next play, Watson glanced briefly toward Larry Ling, his receiver on the right, before he called out, "Two! Four! Ten! Hike!"

The Leopards formed a wall as their quarterback looked for his intended receiver. But deep in the Kudzus' backfield, Ned Bushmiller had Ling covered like wallpaper.

Meanwhile, Terry Gold broke through the

Leopards' line and headed for Watson, who kept fading back.

The beleaguered quarterback searched for a white uniform in the clear. He shifted to the left, then to the right, farther and farther back from the line of scrimmage.

Suddenly, a sea of orange-and-white uniforms was practically on top of him. Before he could position himself to throw the ball, he was brought down — back in his own territory.

From the sidelines, the Kudzus' offense called out to their teammates on the field.

"Way to go!"

"Right on!"

Slaps and cheers rang out as the defense stomped down the field.

"I think they're a little shook up," said Fabian.

Parker agreed. "Wait till we get out there. We'll show 'em a thing or two."

Fabian nodded.

The next play produced a pileup that gained the Leopards nothing.

"Third down and forty? He's gotta throw now," said Spike.

But Watson surprised a Kudzu defense that was looking for the long pass. He flipped a short lateral to his halfback, Albie Fredericks, who looked as though he was in the clear. Fredericks grabbed it, but Billy Wilson, the Kudzus' left tackle, was right there. Billy hit him the minute he took his first step forward.

The ball squirted out of Fredericks's hold and wobbled forward. Mike McCarthy, the Leopards' right guard, and Marty Marino, his Kudzus defensive counterpart, collided as they rushed to pick it up.

Their impact sent the ball bouncing back down toward the east end of the field.

The Kudzu bench was on their feet.

"Get that ball!" rang out from both sides of the field.

After a wild scramble by a dozen players, Kudzu linebacker Jerry Lawrence landed on the ball four-square.

It was on the Leopards' twenty-five yard line!

A chorus of groans broke out in the Leopards' stands. The crowd of Kudzus fans cheered wildly.

This is our big chance, thought Parker. Whoever scores first always has the advantage.

"Let's move that offense!" called Coach Isaac.

"Go, team, go!" shouted the Kudzus fans.

In the huddle, Spike announced his plan of action.

"We're not going to mess up like they did," he said. "We're sticking to the ground. We'll start with Thirty-two Grind."

Just like in practice, thought Parker. Out loud, he said, "Okay, guys, I'll be looking for that hole."

Spike clapped his hands, and the team broke from the huddle.

The Kudzu quarterback barked out the signals. *Wham!* As soon as the ball touched Parker, he was brought down by two Leopard linemen. He barely managed to hold on to the pigskin.

I guess they're wise to that one, he thought.

"Fabe, looks like you're going to have to do it," said Spike. "We'll try Twenty-three Blue."

41

This play called for a quick fake to Parker and then a handoff to fullback Fabian deRosa. It was a play the Kudzus often used at the goal line when they needed just a yard or two.

I guess Spike is planning to crawl down to the goal, Parker thought. As long as we get there.

Huey Walker centered the ball. Spike leaned in, called out, "Two! Zero! Three! Hut! Hut! Hut!"

Spike grabbed the ball, faked toward Parker, then spun around and turned it over to Fabian.

Thud! Again, the Leopards were on top of the receiver. They brought him down almost before he had the ball in his hands.

It was the second loss of yardage for the Kudzus. Now they had twenty-two yards to go for a first down.

"Third and twenty-two," said Cris. "You have to put it in the air, Spike."

"I know, I know," said the Kudzu quarterback. He licked his fingertips. "I'm gonna try one to Moose. We'll go with Eighty-eight Red."

They lined up in their usual single wing position, with Spike behind Huey at center. Fabian stood behind Spike, with Parker to his right and a little forward. Stacy and Cris moved wide to the right and left. Moose got into position just off left tackle.

Spike roared out the signal loud and clear.

The ball was snapped. Spike pulled back a few feet. His protection held. He was able to get off a clean bullet right at Moose.

But it never reached the Kudzus' tight end. A Leopards' player grabbed it in midair and tore off down the field without a Kudzu near him. He crossed the goal line standing up.

The Leopards' center kicked for the extra point and made it. The score: Leopards 7, Kudzus 0.

The kickoff put the Kudzus in good field position again. But their offense ground out three quick plays that went nowhere. There was no choice but to kick back to the Leopards.

"Get some rest," said the coach when Parker got to the bench.

Parker picked up a paper cup and took a drink of water.

Not one single play worked, he thought. Spike didn't seem to be off the mark. He just wasn't getting much of a chance. And whenever he did, it seemed like a Leopard was always there waiting. It's almost as though they knew what we were going to do. Before we did it!

He watched the Leopards move slowly toward the western goal line. Watson, the Leopards' quarterback, wasn't having much luck with his passes, but he had all the time in the world to get them off.

A strange idea began to take shape in the back of Parker's mind.

A roar from the stands interrupted his thoughts. .

Across the field, the Leopards were on their feet cheering. The Leopards had scored again.

But they missed the conversion.

"Go, Kudzus, go!" shouted the fans. They saw a slim chance to get on the scoreboard now. If the Kudzus could make two touchdowns and score the extra points, they could take the lead.

As they lined up for the kickoff, the whistle blew. It was the end of the first quarter.

While the two teams exchanged field positions, the coach called Parker over to him.

"Okay, I want you to listen carefully, Parker," he said. "They'll be looking for you to receive. In the huddle, tell Spike to keep the ball on the ground. Tell him to use Fabian as often as possible."

Parker joined the Kudzus' huddle.

He told Spike what the coach had said.

"Okay, okay," said Spike. "But you guys have to open up those holes. We'll start with Dynamite Black."

Fabian clenched his fist. He was ready to run with the ball.

Again, as soon as the signals were out of Spike's mouth, the Leopards bore down.

This time they stopped Fabian for a loss of five.

On the next down, the Kudzus got lucky. The Leopards were so eager, they were offside before play began.

The penalty gave the Kudzus a little breathing space.

But not enough. Spike handed off to Parker on the next play. He was tackled as soon as he got the ball.

In fact, it felt like the entire Leopard squad was on top of him!

Huey helped him to his feet. "You okay, Parker?" he asked. The short, rugged center was used to pileups. He knew what it felt like to be on the bottom.

Parker brushed the dirt from his hands. He shook off the muscle aches.

"I'm all right," he said. "But something really weird's going on. They're on top of us before we get a chance to run our plays. You know what I think?" he continued. "I think they know them! And this is how. . . ."

He quickly told his teammates about seeing someone run out of Coach Isaac's office with a camera. He described the desk with the open playbook and the gator replica holding it in place.

46

"Then what?" asked Moose.

"The coach came in, and I told him what happened," said Parker.

"Did he say anything? Did he think someone was stealing our plays?" asked Cris.

"Uh . . . not exactly," answered Parker.

"And you never saw the guy's face or anything?" asked Tripp Collins, the Kudzu offensive right guard.

"No, I told you, just his back. 'Sides, he was wearing a hood," said Parker.

"You tried to catch him, but he got away?" asked Huey.

"Yeah, you see, there were a million kids —"

"Parker, you're so full of baloney," Cris interrupted. "When are you going to knock it off and start telling the truth?"

"Hey, we've got a game to play," said Spike.

The referee was starting to pace up and down. They broke from the huddle just in time to avoid a penalty for delaying the game.

Spike had called for a pass to Cris.

Cris pushed past his blocker and raced down the field. As he hit his mark, he turned. He could see the ball spiraling down right at him.

As Cris reached for the ball, a Leopard safety streaked in front of him and grabbed it. Luckily, the receiver went offside right afterward — or there might have been another Leopard touchdown on the scoreboard.

That interception was no lucky break! thought Parker. Their defense knew where Cris was going to be. They always know what we're going to do. It has to be that guy with the camera!

Parker straggled back to the Kudzus huddle.

"Listen, guys, I'm telling you, they know our plays!" he insisted.

But no one paid any attention.

5

The Leopards held on to the ball for most of the second quarter. But the Kudzus defense kept them from scoring again.

At the end of the half, the Leopards were ahead 13–0.

In the locker room, Coach Isaac gave his team a pep talk. "I don't know what's wrong with you guys," he said. "You're making a few mistakes, but there's something else. . . ."

Parker was pretty sure he knew what that something was. But he'd already tried telling the guys, and they had laughed at him. Why should the coach listen?

"You're not connecting. You're always a few seconds behind," the coach continued.

Or the Leopards are a few seconds ahead, thought Parker.

"This half, don't give them an extra inch anywhere," said the coach. "We have to get on the scoreboard fast — build some momentum — really get the steam up. All right, let's see you guys play some football!"

They burst forth from the locker room, an explosion of orange, white, and green. Waiting for play to resume, every Kudzu kept in motion. Shoulder pad connected with shoulder pad. Rubber cleats ground into the dirt as blocks were faked and passes were thrown and caught.

The Kudzus were on the receiving side of the field as the second half started.

The Leopards kicked a low wobbler that went offside just over the midfield mark.

The Kudzus fans cheered the weak kick. There were some boos from the Leopards crowd.

"With great field position, they'll expect a long pass," said Spike. "We'll surprise them. We'll go with Thirty-two Grind."

Again? thought Parker. It hasn't worked yet.

Maybe that's part of the problem. Spike isn't calling a very good game today. Oh, well, I'll do my best.

He never even got a chance.

Before Spike could hand him the ball, the Leopards' nose tackle climbed over Huey and sacked the Kudzus' quarterback. It happened so fast, the ball almost got loose.

"I'm telling you guys . . . ," Parker started to say in the huddle.

But no one was listening to him.

Then Huey reminded them of the new play Coach Isaac had suggested the day before — the backward signal calling for a repeat of the last play.

"They'll never expect it again," he said. "Why don't we give it a try?"

Spike didn't seem to like the idea. But they had to try something a little different.

They lined up for the next play. Spike barked out, "Two! Three! Hut! Hut!"

Huey was right about one thing. The Leopards were slow to react. There was plenty of time to hand off to Parker, time for the offensive line to open a hole, and even a wide-open field once he got clear. He sped down the field and crossed the goal line standing up.

The defense swarmed off the bench and joined their fellow Kudzus surrounding Parker. They hugged so hard, he almost lost his breath.

Meanwhile, the Leopards stood around looking amazed.

That's one you hadn't counted on, thought Parker. You won't find that little switcheroo in the playbook.

When he got to the bench, he tried to talk to Coach Isaac.

"Wait a minute, Parker," the coach said. "Let's see if we make this conversion. Ah, yes!"

More cheers, more high fives, more players coming and going as the Leopards prepared to receive the ball.

Parker never got a chance to tell the coach what he suspected was going on. All the Kudzus were up off the bench for the kick. There was

still time for them to win the game with one more touchdown and conversion.

The Kudzus' kick was a good one. The ball almost reached the goal line before a Leopard snagged it on one short bounce and started downfield. Billy Wilson just managed to bring him down in Leopard territory near the forty-five yard line.

Parker's touchdown had fired up the Kudzus. The defense ground in. It seemed as if every one of their linemen were made of cement blocks. Two attempts at running plays didn't get beyond the line of scrimmage.

The Leopards' quarterback had to take to the air.

"Get that pass!"

"Make that pass!"

The yells from the crowd almost drowned out the sound of the plays being called on the field.

The Leopards weren't about to give up their lead that easily. Their own line dug in. Two short passes put them on the Kudzus' thirty.

"First and ten!" called the referee.

The two teams lined up. It looked as though the Leopards were going to run the ball. There was a handoff to the fullback, who didn't move. Protected by his blockers, he threw a short pass to an open teammate on the far side. There was nothing between the receiver and the goal line but daylight. Touchdown.

With the conversion made, the score now stood at Leopards 20, Kudzus 7.

"Two touchdowns, two touchdowns, and the extra points! We still can do it!" called Rook Stubbs from the far side of the bench. He stood next to the big watercooler, cheering on the players on the field.

"Hey, Spike, how about me?" asked Stacy Fishburne in the huddle. The Leopards' kick had wobbled offside on the Kudzus' thirty. "I haven't seen much of the ball today."

"Yeah, what about Forty-nine Red?" asked Huey. "We practiced that all week."

"Sure," said Spike. "Why not?"

They took their positions. Huey centered the ball. The offensive line held.

Spike looked downfield at Stacy. The Kudzu receiver was just where he was supposed to be.

The pass was a clean spiral straight at the mark. Stacy caught it fair and square. But as he turned to run, two Leopard linebackers hit him crossways and the ball squirted out of his hands.

It bounced around as both teams scrambled to retrieve it.

When the bodies were peeled away from the pileup, a defensive safety for the Leopards was on top of the ball.

The Kudzus offense stomped off the field. The weary defense took over.

"Still time, still time!" called Rook.

But time seemed to be on the side of the Leopards. They didn't eat up much of the clock on their next drive to the goal line.

A short pass from Watson put them in scoring range.

Three running plays in a row followed. Each was good for only a few yards — but a few yards was all they needed. With first and goal to go, Watson himself carried the ball over the mountain of Kudzu linemen. He almost did a somersault as he rose to his feet. The ball was in one hand. The other was clenched in victory.

The Leopards kicked for the conversion, and the score leapt from 20–7 to 27–7. But their offense was looking tired as they jogged off the field.

"They've been on their feet too long," snorted Moose, in the huddle.

"No excuse for us, then," snapped Cris Muldoon. "Let's give their defense something different for a change. Hey, Spike, how about good old Lucky Eighty-seven?"

Lucky Eighty-seven was really just a dressed-up version of the razzle-dazzle that kids played on streets and backyards all over town. It called for a quick round of handoffs and short passes among the three backs before Fabian made a run for it through any hole that was then open. Coach Isaac had just started running it during their final practice the day before the game. It was one of the few plays they had never used in a game before.

"I don't know," said Spike. "We haven't practiced it much."

"Big deal," said Fabian. "That's the beauty.
Doesn't take much practice. Been doin' it as
long as I can remember."

"We have to do something, guys," said Parker.
"They're murdering us."

"Okay," said Spike. "But you guys have to
keep them out of here." He indicated the backfield to the linemen. "We'll go with Lucky
Eighty-seven."

Huey Walker took a deep breath as he
hunched over the ball. Spike crouched behind
him and barked out the signals.

"Ready! Set! Hut! Hut!"

He backed away and handed off to Fabian.

The line held at the center. But from either
end, red-white-and-blue uniforms came at him.

Before he could toss the ball to Parker, he was
tackled.

"Lucky? Hah!" grumbled Spike.

"Maybe we'll get lucky sometime," sighed
Huey.

"We'll go with Slide Twenty-nine," Spike announced.

A draw play. They hadn't made one of those all day. Maybe it would work this time.

It did. But not exactly as planned.

The Leopards were in so fast, Spike dropped the ball. Tripp Collins had made his block when he saw the ball skitter between his legs. He picked it up and realized he was in the clear. Before anyone knew what was happening, he was halfway down the field toward the goalpost. For the first time in his playing career, Tripp had scored a touchdown.

At least he thought he had.

There was a flag down on the field.

A penalty was called: offside — against the Kudzus.

Darren Shultz had moved forward too fast. A glimpse of green and orange just caught the ref's eye.

Tripp almost wept.

"I may never get to cross the goal line with the ball again," he moaned in the huddle.

"Okay, guys, let's try it again," said Spike. "Only let's do it right. Same play."

It was the second time they had tried a replay and, again, it worked. They gained enough yardage for a first down.

Using his runners, Spike managed to gain precious yards, one after another.

Meanwhile, the clock was grinding away.

They were down to the fifteen yard line. Could they go all the way?

Spike called for a short pass to Moose Brogan. If they could get close enough to the goal line, there was a good chance they could score. And a missed pass would stop the clock.

The Kudzus' quarterback had plenty of time to pass, but there were Leopards all over his intended receiver. Suddenly Spike noticed Cris Muldoon in the end zone with no one near him.

He threw the ball in a high arc, and down it came — right into Cris's waiting arms.

The Kudzus wasted no time in celebrating. They lined up and quickly made the conversion.

The scoreboard read Leopards 27, Kudzus 14.

Just one break. That's all they needed. Just one big break.

With so little time left, thought Parker as he jogged toward the bench, our only hope is to get the ball back fast. And maybe come up with some surprises. Unless the Leopards already know every trick in our book!

He had barely reached the sidelines when an onside kick gave the Kudzus their chance. The ball touched one of the Leopards and then bounced into the clear. With a smell of victory in the air, three different Kudzus nearly collided as they pounced on it.

The ball was on the Leopards' forty-five.

First and ten.

Coach Isaac sent Mitch Crum in to replace Fabian deRosa, who was limping. It didn't look serious, but Rook Stubbs took no chances. He helped the Kudzus' fullback into the locker room for a good look at the injury.

"Coach says short passes toward the side-lines," Mitch informed his teammates in the huddle. "Keep stopping the clock."

They had no choice but to follow his strategy.

It might have worked, too, if it weren't for the Leopards' defense. They managed to sack Spike twice in a row.

But he was tough. He got up, called a third-down pass, and managed to connect to Moose. The tight end grabbed the ball and carried it down to the nine yard line. He ran off the side-line just in time to stop the clock with less than a minute to go.

"Come on, guys," shouted Parker. "The Gators can run two sets of plays in less than a minute."

"You and those Gators!" snarled Spike. "Bunch of overgrown lizards!"

"Yeah. Besides, we're not the Gators," said Huey.

Spike called for a screen pass to Mitch, but the ball never left his hand. He was brought down by two Leopards for a loss of five.

And the merciless clock kept ticking.

Without a huddle, the Kudzus lined up for another attempt. This time Spike faked to Parker and handed off to Mitch. The utility back crashed through the line for a few precious yards.

Not enough for a first down.

With only seconds left, the Kudzus got off one last play. Spike tried carrying the ball himself.

He had no more luck than any of his runners.

Final score: Leopards 27, Kudzus 14.

"It's just like they knew our plays better than we did ourselves," said Moose on the way into the locker room. Even so, he wasn't buying Parker's story any more than the rest of the team.

But Parker was more convinced than ever the stranger in the gray hooded sweatshirt had taken pictures of the coach's playbook. Somehow, those pictures had gotten into the Leopards' hands. He was sure of it.

But who was the mysterious person, and why had he done it? And would "Mr. Sweatshirt" be likely to strike again?

6

Parker decided the only way to find the answers to his questions was to stake out the coach's office. That way, he might see if Mr. Sweatshirt reappeared.

But keeping an eye on Coach Isaac's office was more difficult than Parker had imagined. After all, he was supposed to be in class, so he couldn't just skip off whenever he wanted. In between classes, however, he made sure to pass by that doorway as often as he could.

He found ways of leaving classes early, too. He had so many faked coughing fits, the school nurse dragged him into her office and took his temperature.

"Ninety-eight-point-six. I swear, it's the only

normal thing about you, Parker," she joked. "Now, get yourself a drink of water, and back to class with you."

Parked decided the best watercooler to quench his thirst would be the one near the locker room.

It was a lucky choice.

The watercooler was halfway between the equipment room and Coach Isaac's office. As Parker bent over to take a drink, someone came out of the coach's office in a big hurry. That someone was wearing a gray hooded sweatshirt and was dangling something dark and mysterious from one hand.

Parker swallowed a mouthful of water. It almost made him choke for real.

Then he took off after the mysterious stranger, who had just turned the corner into the main corridor. This time there was no after-school crowd. Everyone was still in class.

He had a clear shot and thought of tackling Mr. Sweatshirt. Instead, he tried to grab him from behind.

The next thing he knew, he was sitting on the

floor with an aching arm and a sore rump . . . staring up at Joni!

"You?" he exclaimed.

"You!" she cried. "What were you trying to do, anyhow?"

"I . . . I didn't know it was you. I didn't recognize you," he tried to explain.

"Oh, you just go around grabbing at any girl alone in a corridor," she said angrily. "Good thing we learn about self-defense in gym class."

"You learned it well," said Parker, rubbing his arm. He got up and brushed himself off. "Listen, I can explain everything. Just tell me one thing. What were you doing in the coach's office with a camera?"

"Parker, you are dumb." Joni laughed. "This is my calculator," she said, waving it at him. "We just got through adding up our gymnastics scores, and Ms. Appleton asked me to drop them off. She wants Coach Isaac to see how well we're doing. But what are you doing out of class?"

Boy, do I feel stupid, thought Parker.

"Joni, I'm really sorry," he said. "It's a long

story. I'll see you at lunch and tell you everything."

He did.

Seated at the far end of the cafeteria, he told
her all about the incident a few days ago.

"That mysterious stranger could have been
anyone," she pointed out. "Practically everyone
in this school owns one of those sweatshirts!"

"I know," he groaned. "Just makes it harder.
But I still think it was someone who turned those
pictures over to the enemy."

"Parker, this isn't the Third World War," she
said. "What do you mean 'the enemy?' "

"The Leopards! Joni, I swear they were in on
every one of our plays. We didn't have a chance,"
he said.

"It couldn't have been just a bad day?"

"No way," he insisted. "No, there's a spy in
our midst, I'm telling you. And if we don't find
him —"

"Or her," Joni corrected him.

"Right. Whoever it is could do a lot of damage."

Joni glanced around the cafeteria. She pushed her potato chips to one side of her plate and looked up.

"How do you know it wasn't someone on your own team?" she asked. "After all, any one of the guys would have a good reason to be in the coach's office. Maybe someone forgot a play and needed to have a look at it."

"But with a camera?"

"You thought my calculator was a camera," she reminded him.

"No, it was a camera. I'm sure of it. I saw that automatic flash gizmo gleaming. That's how I know what it was."

"You're absolutely positive?" she asked.

"Uh-huh, and I just wonder if someone didn't sell those pictures to the Leopards. Or to the Mob," he went on.

"Oh, boy, Parker, there you go." Joni sighed. "I wouldn't be surprised if the whole story is just another one of your . . . your . . . *stories!*"

"C'mon, Joni," he said. "I was only trying to

come up with a reason someone would be taking pictures of the coach's playbook."

Joni leaned back in her chair, folded her arms, and scrutinized Parker. "And every single word you told me is the truth?" she said.

"The whole truth and nothing but the truth."

"Well, even I have to admit that it sounds suspicious," she agreed. "But I'm still a little foggy on the . . . uh . . . motive."

"What do you mean?"

"What did the Leopards need your plays for? Didn't they have any of their own?"

"Joni! Come on, think about it. Of course they didn't *use* our plays themselves. But their defense knew what our offense was going to do. That's how they were able to mow us down," he said angrily. "That has to be it."

"Okay, okay," she said, nodding. "So let's just say that someone sneaked into the coach's office —"

"A guy *or* a girl." He smiled.

"Right. And that someone took pictures of the

plays. Hey" — suddenly she stopped — "why didn't they just make photocopies? Would have been a lot easier."

"I thought of that," he said. "But that would have meant taking the playbook out of the office, getting the copies made with nobody watching, and then putting it back without anyone noticing. Too complicated. Too risky."

"That makes sense," she admitted. "And that's how you lost the game with the Leopards. Well, that's that, I guess. Nothing you can do about it now."

"Unless it wasn't just a one-time thing," he said. "Maybe someone is going to steal our plays again."

"You mean the Leopards are going to sell those plays to someone else? I don't get it."

He explained that Coach Isaac came up with a few new plays for each game. They weren't all that different, of course. Some were just simple variations. But anyone who played football knew that old plays weren't worth that much. You had to have the new ones.

"So I think that the spy, or whatever you want to call it," he said, "is going to keep at it."

"Couldn't you tell the coach to keep his playbook locked up?" asked Joni. "I mean, if I wanted to, I could have taken it off his shelf and shot some pictures — with my calculator!" She grinned widely.

"That's not funny, Joni," he said. "This is serious stuff, and if you're not interested —"

"I am, Parker!" she said. "But what can I do?"

"Just keep your eyes and ears open," he said. "I'm going to keep a watch on the coach's office, just like I've been doing."

"All right. Just be careful," she said. "Oh, and one more thing."

"What's that?" he said.

"I'll help you any way I can if . . . if you help me," she said.

"How?"

"Stop by the library after practice and give me a hand studying for my science test."

"What's it on?"

"Take one guess!"

"Reptiles?"

"You win the prize, Parker!"

That afternoon, the polished oak library table was almost covered with books. Several were open, showing pictures of one amphibious creature after another.

Parker explained the minute difference between two types of lizards as Joni rubbed her eyes.

"So you see," he explained, "there's a real family resemblance between these guys and you-know-what."

Joni laughed. "Gators! Of course!"

He reached into his pocket and took out his lucky gator replica. It looked just like the one in the coach's office, only smaller.

"Yep," he said. "And this is the little baby I used to point out a few things to my science class. Now, just take a look at this tail. And these teeth! Isn't he a beaut?"

"Parker, I really think you're obsessed. You'd

probably shoot me if I bought a pair of alligator shoes. Why are you so nuts about gators?"

"Well, it started with my dad," he explained. "See, he played for the Gators, and he might have even turned pro, only he got this knee injury —"

His explanation was interrupted by the heavy tread of some new arrivals in the library.

Spike Newton, Cris Muldoon, and Mitch Crum flopped themselves down at the next table.

"Well, if it isn't the Headless Tailback, playing with his little toy," said Cris.

"Naw, he's got a head — he just left it on the bench —," Mitch started to say.

Cris interrupted, "Naw, in his locker."

"Nope," sneered Spike. "He gave it to his little sister to take home for him."

"You're real funny, guys," said Parker.

"Yeah, a million laughs," added Joni.

"Now, what do we have here?" said Mitch, dragging his chair closer. "Could this be the secret weapon for the legendary Gators, the only college team worth watching according to the expert Parker Nolan?"

"Could that be Parker Nolan, son of the legendary Gators fullback?" added Spike.

"Who would have been an All-Star if —," Cris began, but Joni cut him off.

"I've had it with you knuckleheads," she announced. "*I* have a test coming up."

"Come on," said Parker, getting up from the table. "I'll go over the material on the way home."

The two of them started to leave.

"Oh, Parker," called Mitch after them. "Do you have all your toys?"

Parker didn't bother to reply. But he patted his pocket to make sure the little gator was there.

"Morons," muttered Joni once they were outside.

"Iguana brains," said Parker.

"Isn't that good? Aren't iguanas smart?"

"Not as smart as gators," Parker said with a chuckle.

7

For the next few days, Parker saw hooded school sweatshirts everywhere he looked. Five kids in his own homeroom wore them, including Cris and Spike.

One morning he noticed someone suspicious running out of the principal's office. It turned out to be some kid who was late for gym class.

Later on, another likely suspect showed up in his music class. This time, he found out that the kid had just been too slow to get dressed after gym!

There ought to be a rule that you can't go around the school in a sweatshirt, Parker thought as he sat by himself in the back of the school bus. And then, just as fast, he shook his head. That's not the problem, anyhow.

He just had to catch the spy in the act.

But how? He muddled over several methods of spying.

When Melissa's best friend, Sally, got off the bus, Melissa moved into the empty seat next to him.

"I smell wood burning," she announced. "Parker, you must be thinking!"

"Cute, Melissa, very cute," he said.

"All right, Parker," she said. "I was just kidding. What's going on? Are you still getting grief about your helmet?"

"No, it's not that." He sighed. "I just know I saw someone doing something wrong, you know, committing a crime. But I can't figure out how to prove it, and besides, no one believes me."

"Poor Parker," said Melissa. "It's not as easy as it is on TV, is it?"

"No. But hey — maybe I can get some clues that way," he said. "Thanks, Melissa, you just might have helped."

"Really?"

"Scout's honor," he said.

"Parker! You were never a scout!"

"Parker? What are you doing watching TV before dinner?" asked Mrs. Nolan. She had just gotten home from her part-time job in the town's biggest law office. "Is that some program you're watching for school?"

"No, Mom," he replied. "Just some old detective shows."

"Not for me." She sighed. "I get enough crime at work. You wouldn't believe some of our cases."

"Oh, yeah?" Parker said, suddenly interested. "Does your office deal with a lot of theft and espionage?"

"Theft, yes." Mrs. Nolan smiled. "Espionage is more in the line of the federal government."

"What about stealing secrets?" he went on.

"Well, we have had a few corporate cases that involved stolen designs," she said.

"That's the kind of thing I mean," he said. "What happened? How did they catch the thief?"

"Red-handed, as I recall," Mrs. Nolan said. "Someone came back early from a business trip. He found the thief making off with drawings of a new machine that had just been approved for a trial run."

"What happened to the thief?"

"It hasn't gone to trial yet. Why are you so interested, Parker? You're not thinking about a life of crime, are you?"

"Naw, Mom, come on." He grinned. "Believe me, I'm on the right side of the law."

A lot of people don't believe I saw a crime, Parker thought. I have to prove they're wrong.

The next day, he doubled his effort to keep an eye on the coach's office door.

And so did Joni. That afternoon, they bumped into each other by the watercooler next to the gym.

"Seen anything lately?" he asked between gulps of water.

"Nothing. How about you?"

"Nope."

"Oh, well, I have to go now," she said. "By the way, thanks for the help."

"Help?"

"My science test. Reptiles? Remember? I got an A-plus," she called over her shoulder.

He was glad to hear some good news. Things hadn't been so cheerful during football practice lately.

The loss to the Leopards shouldn't have been that big a deal. The Kudzus had lost games before. But in those cases, it had been easy to see what had gone wrong.

Turnovers. Missed blocks. Plays forgotten. Penalties. There was always something specific to work on afterward.

But the only thing anyone could say about the Leopards game was that they had been "a little bit off."

So each afternoon, the Kudzus had been practicing harder and harder.

And maybe Parker had been trying too hard. He pushed to make up for being a little slow. As a result, he was sometimes a little too fast.

Tweet!

The whistle would blast in his ear.

"Offside!" Coach Isaac had called to him during more than one practice scrimmage. "Parker, wait for the signal!"

The coach hadn't bought his story about someone stealing plays before the last game. But just as he always did, he had put together a new batch of plays for their next game.

Several of those plays had put the ball into Parker's hands. He'd had to learn the play names and numbers, the signals, and the moves. It was a lot of work.

Once in a while everything had come together. He'd remember exactly what he was supposed to do — and so would everyone else. He'd find himself carrying the ball into enemy territory and down the field. It felt great.

Then there were the other times.

He'd move too fast on a handoff and start to run before he had the ball.

Or he couldn't remember the signal.

Instead of keeping his mind on practice, he kept thinking about someone stealing plays.

Who?

Why?

And would it happen again?

8

Parker also found his mind wandering in school. One day, he got so wound up in his thoughts, he almost walked by his own locker. History class was over, and that was one heavy book. He decided to put it away.

It didn't take much concentration to dial his combination — nineteen, seven, two — the year the Gators had won their last conference title.

As he dumped the history book on the top shelf, a heavy chunk of green metal fell down and nearly hit him.

He picked it up.

It was a gator! A green metal gator!

In fact, it was the same one he'd seen on top

of the coach's playbook the practice before the Leopards game.

How did it get there? He was the only person in the whole school who knew the combination to his locker. He had set it himself.

And he never, absolutely never, left his locker open.

The only other way to get into student lockers was with the master key in the principal's office. The principal always made a big thing out of it when he had to use it in an emergency. Parker would have known if that had happened.

No, it had to be someone who knew how to crack a combination lock. But who? And why would he have chosen to put the gator in Parker's locker?

One thing was for sure: he had to return the gator replica. And he had to tell the coach where he'd found it.

Parker hurried down to the coach's office.

The door was open. Coach Isaac was sitting behind his desk with one hand on the telephone.

Parker walked in and handed him the gator.

"Coach!" said Parker, all excited. "Look what I just found in my locker!"

"You *found* it *where?*" asked Coach Isaac.

"In my locker," said Parker. "I was just putting my history book away and —"

"Parker, that's the second time I've seen you holding my paperweight. What on earth was it doing in your locker?" asked the coach angrily. "I thought it had been stolen. As a matter of fact, I was just about to report it to the principal's office."

"I don't know how it got there, Coach," Parker said. "I always keep my locker locked. No one has the combination. But someone put it there, I swear."

"Well, I'm sure that if you had stolen it, you wouldn't be bringing it back," said Coach Isaac. "It's probably some stupid prank. You must have left your locker open. While you weren't looking, someone put it in. But whoever it was had no right to take it from here. Was this some kind of a dare you guys were up to?"

"No, Coach, I swear —," Parker insisted.

"You don't have to swear, Parker," the coach replied. "I believe you . . . this time. You may, well, *stretch the truth* once in a while, but you're no thief. Say, shouldn't you be in class now?"

Parker was late. He left the coach's office and ran off to his math class.

When he got there, they had already finished going over the previous day's homework.

"Nice of you to join us, Parker," said Ms. Cobertson as he quietly took his seat. "May I have your homework, please?"

Parker reached for his notebook to find the assignment. But his notebook wasn't there. Had he lost it?

Or had it been stolen?

As he fumbled to come up with an explanation, he saw everyone staring at him.

Staring — and laughing.

Did he have his shirt on backward or something?

Parker felt something nudge him at the elbow.

Cris Muldoon was standing there, waving a

brown leather three-ring binder with P.N. in big gold letters on it.

"Uh, where was it?" he whispered to Cris.

"You left it on your seat back in homeroom, dummy," said Cris. "I figured I'd give it to you before class, but you weren't around."

"Thanks," said Parker. He handed in his paper.

"Now perhaps we can get on with today's lesson," said Ms. Cobertson. "Let's all take a look at page forty-three. . . ."

Parker had been a whiz in math class that year. For the first time, everything about it had made sense. He didn't even need a pencil and paper or a calculator. He could do most of it in his head.

But lately, even the simplest problem was beyond him. His hand used to shoot up into the air whenever Ms. Cobertson asked the class a question. Now he almost never lifted it off his desk.

In fact, he just couldn't seem to concentrate on any of his schoolwork these days. Instead, he'd take out a sheet of paper and draw elaborate doodles — zigzags and scribbles and all sorts of things that popped into his wandering mind.

As Ms. Cobertson put down a series of math problems on the blackboard, he took out a piece of paper and started to doodle on top.

He did it automatically, without thinking. In fact, that's what he'd been doing earlier in homeroom. No wonder he forgot his binder. Too busy scribbling and drawing doodads. And stopping off at his locker to dump his history book.

As Parker's attention wandered, one of the doodles started to look like a locker. He drew numbers blasting off from it, like in a comic book.

Suddenly, Parker sat up. He remembered drawing a similar picture in homeroom. Maybe that's how someone got my combination! he thought. Anyone could have been looking over my shoulder. So that's how someone got into my locker. Someone who knows I'm a big Gators fan, too! Gosh, everyone knew about that.

But who would do that — set me up with a stolen gator?

Cris?

Too obvious. Why would Cris have made such a big show of giving him the lost notebook? No, it had to be someone else. Someone who also snagged the gator from the coach's office.

Joni? She certainly knew how much he liked gators. Wait a minute. That was ridiculous. She hadn't even known about the guy with the camera until he told her about it.

The more he thought about it, the more an ugly picture took shape in his mind.

It couldn't be. It just couldn't be.

9

That afternoon, Parker was more distracted than ever during practice. He kept looking around as if he might see something. Maybe someone wearing a gray hooded sweatshirt would simply walk up to him, point a camera at him, and shout, "Surprise!" What if it was all some kind of joke, like one of those weird hidden video TV shows?

If only it were that simple, he thought as he missed a lateral.

"Parker, are you playing football or searching for UFOs?" called the coach from the bench. "Let's see some heads-up ball!"

"Better get with it, Parker, or you'll be warming the bench," said Cris.

"Okay, okay! Spike, let me try Thirty-two Grind for a change. Haven't done much with it since the Leopards game."

"Aw, Parker, you don't want to get hurt, do you?" asked Spike. "This is just a scrimmage. Save it for the real game."

"C'mon, Spike," Parker pressed. "I want to keep in shape. Give me the ball."

"All right," Spike agreed.

This time the play worked like clockwork. Parker broke through the small hole in the line. He wove his way through the secondary defense into the clear. Since it was just a practice session, he didn't run all the way down to the goal line, but awfully close.

It felt good to get something right that day.

After practice, he stopped by Joni's house on his way home. He told her about the gator in his locker and his visit to the coach's office. He showed her the doodle in his three-ring binder.

He was about to tell her his latest theory when

she suddenly blurted out, "It has to be someone on the team!"

"The perpetrator?"

"Exactly! The perp!"

"That's what I've been thinking, too," he admitted reluctantly. "But I just can't believe it."

"Why not?" she asked.

"Well, for one thing," he said, "we all know the plays. We don't have to steal them from the coach's playbook."

"All of them?"

"Sure, and we go over and over and over each one," he explained. "Any one of us could draw those plays from memory."

"You really think so?"

She paused, as if an idea were forming in her mind.

"Okay," she said. "Prove it."

"Prove what?" he asked.

"Prove you can draw the plays from memory. Draw one."

"Joni, this is silly," he protested.

"I'm serious," she insisted. "Go ahead and draw one, any one."

He took out a fresh piece of loose-leaf paper from the back of his binder and started to draw.

First he marked all the positions at the line of scrimmage with the starting team's numbers. Then he drew a dotted line to indicate where he would move when the signal was given.

"See?" he asked.

"Mmmmmm," she said. "That's one where you get the ball and carry it. Draw one where you don't have anything to do."

"I *always* have something to do," he said. "But I know what you mean. I'll draw a pass play where I don't get the ball."

He started out fine, but when it came to marking what Spike did and where the receiver moved, he couldn't quite remember.

He tried another, and it was worse. He couldn't recall much of what anyone else did, where they hit a mark — anything that didn't directly involve him.

"See?" she said. "You can't be sure what everyone else has to do. No one on the team can. So making copies of what you know would be only part of the picture."

"Those Leopards knew every move to all our plays," he said. "They had to have copies of them."

"What could be more natural than one of the players dropping by the coach's office before practice? It would be easy enough for him to snap the pictures and then get lost in the after-school crowd."

"All right, all right," he admitted. "It could have been one of the guys on the team. But why? And which one?"

10

That evening, Parker decided to take a scientific approach to his investigation. On a piece of paper, he jotted down a team roster. Every member was a suspect.

Then, along the top of another page, he made some column headings — possible motives:

"Was bribed"
"Hates the coach"
"Hates school"
"Hates the rest of the team"
"Is just plain stupid"

Then he made a column titled "Has acted suspicious."

There was plenty of space under each column

for the names of suspects to be penciled in. He left room for additional bits of information, too. He'd keep his eyes and ears open and ask Joni and Melissa to do the same.

To start off, there weren't any names in any of the columns. Then, day by day, the spaces started to fill up.

"Darren Shultz was late for practice," Parker wrote in the "Has acted suspicious" column. He added, "Could have been in the coach's office while we were all out on the field."

Then Joni found out that Darren had been taking a makeup history test.

The next item went under the "Hates the rest of team" column: "Fabian deRosa complained he never gets any help."

But that was soon followed by: "Fabian scored three times in practice, then announced, 'I couldn't have done it without you guys.' "

Most of the offense and a large part of the defense came in for comments, one after the other. But then explanations followed, and the comments were crossed out.

At the same time, a lot of comments were being made about Parker — by his teachers.

"Haven't finished the assignment, Parker?"

"Lost your homework?"

"Don't know the answer?"

"Can't find the place? Will someone please show Parker where we're reading!"

The grades on his papers went from A's to B's to C's, one after another.

But Parker hardly noticed. His mind was definitely elsewhere.

Then Parker decided to take another approach to his investigation.

"Mom," he asked one morning, "remember how you said I could use the computer in your office for homework? Can I come by after practice?"

"That won't give you much time before I have to come home," said Mrs. Nolan. "Can't you use one of the computers in school?"

"This is kind of private stuff," he explained. "It won't take much time."

"Well, it *is* the best time," she said. "The office is pretty quiet late in the day. All right — I'll see you later."

That afternoon, Parker entered all his information into a program on his mom's computer. He added a new list next to each player's name — his best guess for what the chances were that that person was the perpetrator.

Cris Muldoon: 50–50
Spike Newton: 50–50
Fabian deRosa: 50–50
Morris Comer: 50–50

Parker hoped that this program would sort all the information and spit out the name of the most likely suspect. But when he tried to make the program work, nothing much happened. The computer just alphabetized the list of player's names.

He figured he'd just have to keep at it. He

decided to add new information every day. Whenever he picked up the slightest clue, he changed the odds. This meant stopping by Mrs. Nolan's office every day after practice.

One afternoon, he came in almost breathless with excitement. Joni had just told him that she'd seen Fabian deRosa coming out of the FotoQuick shop. A solid clue!

He rushed to change the odds next to Fabian's name. Then he punched in every combination of keys he knew. But the computer just gave him the same alphabetized list every time.

Later that day, Joni called to say that her friend Gloria told her that Fabian had bought the nicest photo album for his mother's birthday. With a sigh, Parker changed back the odds after Fabian's name.

"Isn't this secret math project taking a lot of time?" asked Mrs. Nolan during dinner a few days later. "I don't seem to hear anything about History or Science or any of your other subjects."

Parker stared at the vanilla ice cream melting away on the pecan pie in front of him.

"I'll eat that if you don't want it, Parker," offered Melissa.

"Parker? You didn't answer me," said Mrs. Nolan. "Are you all right?"

"Oh, I'm fine," he said, grabbing the pie plate back from Melissa. He started gobbling the ice cream. "Just have a lot on my mind. Big project for the science fair."

"The science fair was last month," said Melissa.

"Next year's fair!" snapped Parker. "Can't start too soon."

"Paaaarkerrrr." His mother frowned. "What's going on?"

"Okay, you might as well know, too," he said. "I'm pretty sure I saw someone stealing something."

"Did you report it?" asked Mrs. Nolan.

"I tried to, but no one believed me," Parker explained. "I didn't see who it was and . . . well, there's no real absolutely positive proof, but I'm sure of it. And if I can just find out who it is, then, well, then everyone will see that I've been telling the truth."

"I'm sure that's important, Parker," said his mother. "But you have to be very careful about accusing someone unless there's no doubt whatsoever."

"I know that, Mom," he said.

"And your first responsibility is to your schoolwork. Playing Dick Tracy is one thing, but you mustn't neglect your studies."

But he was. In class, when he was called on, he sometimes didn't even know what the question was.

Even worse, his weekly tests were being affected. Math was usually his best subject. But at the end of that week, he got such a low test score, it brought his average way down.

"I'm sorry, Parker," said Ms. Cobertson as she handed him the test after class, "but your average is below the passing level. You cannot participate in athletics. At least not until you bring up your average. I'll have to leave a note for Coach Isaac in his mailbox."

Parker was stunned. The Kudzus were scheduled to play their biggest rival, the Pittstown Piranhas, that Saturday. He had to play. He couldn't miss the most important game of the year.

Besides, it was a chance to get a close look at the team in action. He was sure to pick up more clues.

He stared down at the math test with the failing grade. It was the worst mark he'd ever gotten. How was he going to explain it to his mother? To the coach? To everyone?

"So, is Parker Nolan the math genius everyone thinks he is?"

The deep voice asking the question belonged to Huey Walker. He and Mitch Crum crowded around Parker's desk, trying to see the grade.

"Yeah, what did you get on that test?" asked Mitch.

"Leave me alone," said Parker angrily. "Don't be so nosy."

"Hey, you guys, you expect him to tell you the truth?" Spike Newton called from the doorway. "How can you trust a guy who lies — and steals?"

"Bug off!" Parker shouted. "All of you, just get off my case."

They just won't let up on anything, he thought. And wait until they hear I can't play.

Then another thought occurred to him.

Who says anyone has to hear?

Ms. Cobertson said she was going to leave a note for the coach in his mailbox. But it was the last class of the day — and it was Friday. The way the school delivered mail, Coach Isaac wouldn't get anything until Monday.

No one said I have to tell him I can't play, Parker thought. I don't have to say anything to anyone.

And what's the big deal about a stupid math test, anyway?

Especially since I think I know now who was in the coach's office with the camera that day.

103

11

Knowing who had done it was one thing. Proving it was another.

Short of catching the perp in the act again, Parker thought, there *has* to be a way to trip up the guilty individual.

That evening after supper, he tried to come up with a plan.

"Melissa, will you please stop shuffling those cards?" he asked. "I'm trying to concentrate."

"Okay, Parker, I'll put them away if you're not interested in playing," she said.

She reached over and slipped the deck into a small brown envelope with a clasp.

"Where's their box?" he asked.

"Got lost," she said. "This is just as good."

Almost as good as the real thing, he thought. Suddenly, his whole face lit up.

Oh, boy, he thought. What a great idea! But would it work?

He headed for the telephone.

"Hi, Joni? Got a minute? I want to talk something over with you. What do you think of this?"

It was bitter cold that Saturday. Gray clouds hovered over the field.

Parker hunkered down on the sideline to watch the coin toss.

"We might even get some snow today," he heard Rook Stubbs say.

"Brrrrr," said Coach Isaac, clapping his gloved hands. "Better make sure that drinking water doesn't freeze."

The Kudzus won the toss and elected to receive. The Piranhas' placekicker booted the ball high into the darkening sky. But it didn't travel very far downfield. Perry McDougal, the Kudzus' back-up offensive running back, was on the special team that received. He was in the clear for a moment as the ball came toward him. He looked like he was thinking about running it. Then a wall of Piranhas was suddenly bearing down on him. Wisely, he signaled for a fair catch.

"Good going, Perry," said Cris as the Kudzus' regular offense came onto the field.

The eleven players gathered into a tight huddle, stomping to keep warm in the frosty air. As Spike started to speak, Parker leaned way in, his elbows almost touching the ground. A yellow FotoQuick envelope dropped onto the frozen turf in front of him.

"Whoops!" he said loudly.

He picked it up and made a big show of stashing it inside his uniform, under his protective padding.

"What's that?" asked Huey.

"Oh, just some interesting pictures," said Parker. He glanced around the huddle very mysteriously.

"Pictures?" asked Cris. "What kind of pictures? And what are you doing with pictures here?"

He sounded real bothered.

"I just found them in the locker room before the game," Parker explained.

"Well, what did you bring them out here for?" sneered Moose.

"Remember what I told you during the game with the Leopards? How I saw someone with a camera coming out of Coach's office? Well, I finally figured out who that someone was." He patted the pictures and smiled knowingly.

"How'd you figure that out?" asked Cris.

"Never mind," said Parker.

"Oh, for crying out loud," said Spike. "This is just another one of Parker's stories."

"Yeah, Tall-Tale Nolan strikes again," added Fabian. "Come on, let's play ball."

"Okay, we'll go with Thirty-two Red," said Spike. "Let's see if Parker can block as well as he talks."

The new version of the old Thirty-two Grind called for a fake to Parker then a pass to Moose Brogan.

Spike crouched down behind Huey.

"Three! Zero! Two! Hike!" he yelled.

Before he could take two steps backward, the Piranhas had broken through the line. The play collapsed in a jumble of bodies with Spike and the ball on the bottom.

The Kudzus' quarterback brushed off the dirt.

With the rest of the offense gathered around, he announced, "We'd better keep it on the ground. Fabe, we'll go with Super Seventy-six."

This was Coach Isaac's version of an old Statue of Liberty play. Spike would raise his arm high, as if he were getting ready to pass. Fabe would sweep by him, grab the ball, and then run for it.

For the play to work, though, Fabian had to make his block and then move fast.

They'd gone over it again and again in practice. And even after the Kudzus' own defense had figured out the play, somehow it usually worked.

This time it didn't.

The minute Spike called the signals, the Piranhas broke through the line. They were all over Fabian in seconds.

Spike had kept his wits about him. He decided to try to run with the ball, but half the Piranhas' defense was ready for him. They brought him down for a loss of five.

Third and fifteen.

After another failure to put a runner through the Piranhas' line, the Kudzus were forced to give up the ball.

As the defense took over, Parker trotted off the field.

"What's with those pictures, Parker?" Moose asked. "You going to let us see them?"

"Why should I?" said Parker. "You guys think you know everything."

A few of the other guys asked him about the yellow envelope. Huey said he ought to "put up or shut up" about his claim that they were pictures of the Kudzus' plays.

"Let's just watch the game, okay?" Parker said, turning his attention to the field.

The Piranhas' quarterback threw a screen pass to his tight end. But a Kudzu linebacker cut him down the minute he started to run. The impact shook the ball loose, and a Kudzu fell on it.

The turnover sent the Kudzus' offense right back onto the field.

The ball was on the Piranhas' thirty-five yard line.

"What a lucky break!" yelled Rook Stubbs. "Okay, you guys, go for it!"

"Parker? Fabian?" barked Spike in the huddle. "Are you guys ready to play some ball? We're going to keep it on the ground. You'll have your work cut out for you."

"Just try me," said Parker.

"Me, too!" said the burly fullback.

"Okay, first let's try an end-around. Number Seventy-two."

This was Fabian's play, and he made the most of it. Even though the Piranhas moved in on him, he managed to break through for a gain of five yards.

It was all the yardage the Kudzus got. At every

one of the following plays, they were stopped cold.

"Rats! That defense is reading us like *See Spot Run*," snarled Cris as they came off the field.

"Yeah, only this Spot isn't doing much running," grumbled Moose.

Parker just shook his head.

The Piranhas got their own lucky break on the very first down. The quarterback passed to his wide receiver deep in Kudzu territory, but the ball squirted out of his hands. It bounced behind him toward the goal line. The Piranhas' tight end was in the right place at the right time. He picked it up just inside the five-yard marker. A little screen pass put the Piranhas on the scoreboard.

The kick for the extra point was good. With the clock signaling the end of the first period, the score was Piranhas 7, Kudzus 0.

When the offense took over, Parker spoke up.

"Listen, you guys," he said. "We can't keep running these plays. They know them. I'm telling you, they know our signals."

"So what do you expect us to do?" asked Cris. "Make up new plays?"

"No, just change signals," said Parker.

"Like the pros?" asked Moose. "We've never practiced that kind of thing."

"We can do it," Parker insisted. "We can."

He quickly outlined a simple plan. They would make the changes one play at a time.

"Don't I have something to say?" snapped Spike. "We can't do it. It's going to be too hard to remember."

"I think we ought to give it a try," said Fabian. "I'm tired of banging my head against a wall."

"I think it's a good idea," said Morris Comer, the usually silent left guard. "We have to do something."

Spike hemmed and hawed.

Tripp, too, seemed doubtful.

But in the end, those who agreed with Parker were louder and stronger than those opposed. The doubters finally had to go along with the idea.

The first time they tried it, Spike messed up

the signal. An offside penalty was called against the Kudzus.

"See, it isn't going to work," he said.

"Come on, Spike," said Cris. "Give it a fair shot."

They tried it again. And again, there was confusion. But this time, both sides got things mixed up — and it turned out well for the Kudzus. They gained seven yards.

"Maybe that's the way. Just keep messing up and see what happens," joked Fabian back in the huddle.

"No, we have to get it straight," insisted Parker.

Once more they tried the last-minute switch. This time it worked like a precision engine.

Spike had more time to position himself. His pass to Cris was right on the mark. Cris was all by himself. Before he was brought down by a Piranha safety, he had gained twenty-five yards.

The Kudzu offense was in Piranha territory for the first time that day.

12

The guys on the bench were jumping up and down with excitement.

It carried over to the field.

By switching signals at the last minute, the offense stormed down the gridiron. In just four quick plays, they crossed into the end zone for their first score.

The talented toe of Huey Walker made the conversion good.

The scoreboard now read: Piranhas 7, Kudzus 7.

The kick to the Piranhas wasn't that great, but it kept them in their own territory.

"Okay, defense, it's your turn!" shouted Coach Isaac. "Spike, get some rest." Then, in the next breath, he asked Spike, "What's going on out there?"

Spike explained the change.

"I never would have figured you guys could do it," said the coach. "But I'm glad it's working. Might as well keep it up."

Meanwhile, the Piranhas were in control of the ball.

They were playing it a little safer. Their quarterback kept the ball on the ground as much as possible.

Even though the Kudzus defense was fired up, the Piranhas managed to grind out yard after yard. After three first downs, they were within striking distance of the goal.

But with ten to go on the Kudzus' thirty, they tried a draw play that misfired.

The Kudzus defense broke through for the blitz and a seven-yard loss.

The next play produced even worse results for the Piranhas. A pass to their wide receiver was intercepted by Ned Bushmiller. The Kudzu safety ran with it until he was forced offside on the enemy's forty yard line.

The crowd went wild.

The offense grabbed their helmets and rushed onto the field. Biting cold wind and frost on the hard ground meant nothing. They could smell a chance at victory.

There was no question about what the Kudzu offense had to do. It would be Parker's system, one play at a time.

If the Piranhas got wise, they could always shift back to their regular signals.

They didn't have to.

On the very first play, Spike slipped the ball into Fabian's hands. The waiting fullback sprung forward. At the line, Tripp Collins and Darren Shultz had opened a big hole for him. He sped through it into the Piranhas' backfield, where he was brought down. It was a gain of eight yards.

On the next play, Spike spun around and shoved the ball into Parker's waiting hands. Parker raced toward Moose. The Kudzus' tight end blocked his man and cleared the way for the charging tailback.

It was all the daylight Parker needed. With lightning-quick moves, he wove his way through the few Piranhas left standing. He sped down-field and crossed the goal line.

Stacy was the first to reach him. The wide receiver gave him a big hug. The rest of the team followed with slaps on the back, high fives, and cheers.

They got into position for the conversion. Huey kicked a wobbler. It just made it into fair territory to put the Kudzus ahead, 14–7.

But as the play cleared, Parker rolled over on the ground. He started to get up, then fell back, clutching his leg.

Rook Stubbs ran onto the field with his black leather bag.

"What's the matter, Parker?" he asked.

"It's my ankle," said Parker. "It hurts some-thing awful."

He tried to get up, then groaned.

"Just take it easy," said Stubbs. He carefully felt around the area and asked a few questions.

"I don't think it's broken. Probably just a bad sprain. Can't really tell much out here," he said. "We'd better get you off the field. Think you can make it with some help?"

"I'll . . . I'll try." Parker groaned.

Stubbs waved over Tripp and Darren, who were standing nearby. They got on either side of Parker and boosted him up gently. Leaning on them, he hopped off the field on one leg.

There was a big cheer from the crowd as he reached the bench. Out of the corner of his eye, he thought he saw Joni clapping her hands.

"What do you think, Rook?" asked Coach Isaac.

"Don't really know yet," said Stubbs. "Give me a few minutes."

The coach nodded and turned back to watch the action on the field.

Rook gingerly removed the rubber-cleated shoe from Parker's foot. Parker winced and clenched his fists.

"Does that hurt?" asked Rook, poking just above the ankle.

"A little," said Parker. "But I'm really freezing, too." He shuddered and shook. "The half's almost over. Maybe . . . maybe we could go in and warm up."

"Yeah," agreed Stubbs. "We could do that. I'll get a couple of guys to give you a hand."

"No!" Parker hissed in a loud whisper. "I don't want anyone to think I'm a wimp. I'm sure I can make it by myself if I just lean on you a little."

"Sure," Stubbs said, nodding toward the team on the bench. "They're all watching the game. No one will notice. We'll take it real slow and easy."

Leaning on the sturdy trainer, Parker hopped off into the locker room.

"Now, let's take a good look at that ankle," said Stubbs.

"It's really okay," said Parker. "Look, I can stand on it."

"Careful!" shouted Stubbs. "You might do some damage."

"No, really," said Parker. He jumped up and down on one foot, then the other.

"That's the fastest comeback I've ever seen," said Stubbs, scratching his head. "Wait a minute! Parker, were you faking it?"

"Yes, I was," Parker admitted. "But, you see —"

"Parker Nolan, I'm fed up with your —"

"Please, Mr. Stubbs, this is no lie. I mean, there's a reason I faked getting hurt. It's for the good of the team, I swear. And I promise you, I'll be able to explain everything if you just trust me. Besides, when they see me on my feet, everyone will think you're a miracle worker," said Parker. "All I ask is one favor, one tiny favor."

"I don't care about credit for something I didn't have anything to do with," said Stubbs. He sighed. "Okay, Parker. Just tell me what's on your mind."

"Well, uh, you know there's been a lot of funny stuff going on lately," said Parker.

"What do you mean, 'funny stuff'?" asked Stubbs.

"I mean how we've been getting murdered out there by their defense. Seems like the last couple of games, they know our plays almost better than we do."

"Don't be so hard on yourself, Parker. And on the other guys," said Stubbs.

"I mean it," Parker insisted.

He told Stubbs about seeing someone come out of the coach's office with a camera and then run off.

"That's when we started losing so badly," he pointed out. "Today, when we started changing signals at the line, you saw how it went."

Stubbs scratched his head.

"You have a point there," he admitted.

"I also have a plan," said Parker. "But there isn't much time. All you have to do is stay behind that back row of lockers with me."

"That's all? For how long? First half's almost over. The guys'll be pouring in here."

"It won't be long," said Parker.

"I don't know . . . ," Stubbs said, hesitating.

"I promise — all we have to do is stay quiet back there for a few minutes."

"All right." Stubbs sighed. "Here, let me give you a hand."

Without thinking, Parker started limping toward the locker.

"Wait a second. You don't need any help. There's nothing wrong with your ankle!" scolded the trainer.

"Whoops!" said Parker. "I almost forgot."

13

As they huddled behind the last row of lockers, Parker and Stubbs could hear the field announcer.

"Second and ten, the ball is on the Piranhas' own forty."

"Third and eight."

"One minute left to go in the period."

"Penalty against the Kudzus. The Piranhas have an automatic first down."

There were just a few seconds remaining when the door to the locker room slammed open.

Parker and Stubbs heard someone enter and stomp toward a locker.

The locker door clanged open.

"They're still here!" boomed an angry voice.

"Let's go!" hissed Parker to Stubbs.

The two of them rushed out from their hiding place.

They came around the corner and saw Spike Newton holding a yellow FotoQuick envelope. He was scratching his head and staring at its contents.

As soon as he saw Parker and Stubbs, Spike tried to stow the envelope back in his locker.

But it was too late.

"What's the matter? 'Fraid to let anyone see your little pictures?" sneered Parker.

"Let me just take a look there," said Stubbs. He took the envelope from Spike and pulled out the contents.

Just as Parker suspected, there were the photographs of the Kudzus' plays.

"What are you doing with these, Spike?" asked Stubbs.

"I . . . I was having trouble remembering the plays, so . . . so I got these from the coach's playbook," the Kudzus' quarterback stammered. "And what about you?" he suddenly

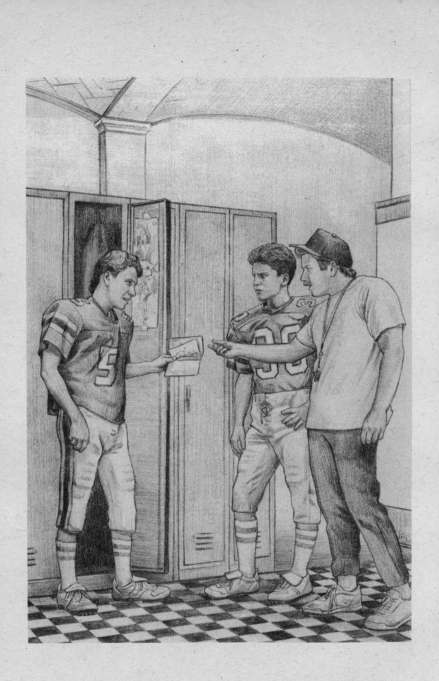

snapped at Parker. "What's in that envelope you dropped in the huddle?"

Parker pulled the envelope out from under his pads. He handed it to Stubbs.

The trainer removed its contents — a bunch of blank index cards.

"You tricked me, you rat!" cried Spike. "I thought you had found my pictures. But it doesn't mean anything. Like I said, I forgot my plays and —"

A whistle blasted outside, followed by a loud roar.

Then, with a clatter of cleats and slapping of pads, the Kudzus burst into the locker room.

Coach Isaac spotted his quarterback, tailback, and trainer. "What's going on here?" he asked. "Is this a private huddle?"

Spike began to protest his innocence, but Stubbs stopped him. He told the story he had put together from what Parker had said and what he had seen with his own eyes. "You be the judge, Coach," he finished.

There was silence in the locker room. Everyone had quieted down. They were all listening to hear what the coach would say.

"No," Coach Isaac replied. "I'm not going to make any judgments. I'm going to ask one question."

He stared Spike straight in the eye. The quarterback hunched his shoulders and bent his head down.

Very softly, the coach asked, "Spike, did you take pictures of my playbook and do something wrong with them?"

So quietly that you could hardly tell that he had spoken, Spike answered after a pause, "Yes, sir."

"Thank you for telling me the truth, Spike," the coach went on. "Now, can you tell me what you did with the pictures?"

"I . . . I loaned them," said Spike. "To some other teams."

"Other teams?"

"You know — the Leopards, the Piranhas."

"And what do you mean 'loaned' them?"

"I let them borrow them and make copies. And then they gave them back."

Coach Isaac sighed a deep sigh.

"Why did you 'loan' our plays to our opponents, Spike?"

It seemed like forever before the red-faced quarterback replied.

"They gave me money for them."

"So, you *sold* our plays," said the coach.

"Yes, sir," said Spike. "I . . . I needed money, for lunch and stuff. My dad got laid off, and my family doesn't have much money. . . ."

Spike wasn't the only one staring down at the floor now. The other Kudzus felt pretty bad hearing his story.

He went on. "Then one of the guys on the Leopards bumped into me and offered me a lot of money if I could get copies of our plays for them to see. He even gave me this little camera. It's in my regular locker upstairs."

"What about the Piranhas?" the coach asked.

"The guy on the Leopards told one of them

about it. Then he got in touch with me and offered the same deal," Spike said.

"It was just one of the guys each time?" asked Coach Isaac. "Not their coach or anyone else connected with the team?"

"No, sir," said Spike.

"So that's why you never wanted to try any new plays!" said Huey.

"I kept thinking you hated taking anyone else's suggestions," said Cris. "Never could figure out why, though."

"I . . . I didn't want to double-cross those guys who got the plays from me," Spike admitted.

"What a mess!" said Coach Isaac. "And no one would ever have known if —"

"If this youngster hadn't gone and twisted his ankle!" said Stubbs, clapping Parker on the back.

14

P arker took a deep breath before speaking. "That's not exactly true," he admitted. "I didn't hurt my ankle, Coach. I . . . I set Spike up."

"You what?"

Parker explained his little plot to get Spike to look for the pictures. He showed his own FotoQuick envelope with the blank cards.

"How did you know it was someone on the team?" asked Rook Stubbs.

"At first, I didn't know who it was," said Parker. "But even though no one believed me, I *did* see someone with a camera run out of your office, Coach."

"You thought it was Spike? You didn't say so

when you told me about the incident," Coach Isaac said.

"I didn't know who it was," Parker repeated. "It happened so fast. I just saw this blur of a person in a gray sweatshirt. It wasn't until later that I thought it was Spike."

"Why?" asked the coach.

"Remember that paperweight?"

"The gator?" asked the coach. "You said you found it in your locker."

"Yes, sir," Parker continued. "And that same day, after I brought it back to you, Spike mouthed off to me in class. He said, 'How can you trust a guy who lies — *and steals!*' I never stole anything in my life. No one can say I did!"

"Ah, so when he said that, you figured he set you up to look like a thief." Stubbs nodded.

"Lying's just as bad as stealing." Spike sniffed.

"We'll let someone else be the judge of that, young man," said the coach sternly. "Get dressed and wait outside. It'll be up to the school authorities to see what's to be done with you. Rook, see if you can get in touch with the principal."

When Spike had left, Coach Isaac turned his attention back to the team.

"Mitch, you'll have to take over —," he started to say when Parker interrupted him.

"Uh, Coach, uh, there's one more thing I ought to tell you," said Parker.

"Who else has a copy of our plays?" Coach Isaac sighed.

"No, it's not that. It's something else," said the young tailback.

He told the coach about his failing grade in math. And, more important, he confessed that he should have told him about it before the game.

"That means you're ineligible to play today," said the coach.

"Yes, sir," admitted Parker. "I would have told you, but I had to be here to find out who the thief was. It's the only way I could prove I wasn't lying and . . . well, you know, help out."

"Parker, I'm not sure that was the only way or the best way," said the coach. "I do believe, however, that you were honest about wanting to help out. Still, I have to abide by the school rules. You're suspended for the rest of the game."

"I understand," said Parker.

"You can stay in uniform and watch the second half from the bench," said the coach.

"Some game it's going to be without our starting quarterback — and now our tailback, too," groaned Stacy.

"Hey, guys," said Coach Isaac, "what's the matter with you? Are you all a bunch of cream puffs? Or are you football players?"

"Let's go!" they shouted.

"Let's hit that field and show them that we can play fair and win!"

The locker room walls almost burst from the explosion of cheers that rang out. The Kudzus were ready to give Coach Isaac their answer loud and clear.

Parker straggled out after the rest of the team.

"What about the youngster on the Piranhas who paid Spike? And the one on the Leopards?" he asked Coach Isaac.

"Oh, I'm sure we'll find out who they were,"

answered the coach. "The authorities will deal with them eventually."

"But what about today's game?" Parker asked.

"I don't think that knowing our plays will do them much good," said the coach. "Once they see that Spike is gone, they'll know they're in trouble. I suspect that will be enough to even up the odds."

"Well, it sure will make for a different kind of game." Parker smiled. "I can't wait for the rest of this one."

15

When Coach Isaac and Parker came out of the locker room, Parker planted himself down at the far end of the bench.

"No way," shouted Mitch Crum. The new acting quarterback grabbed Parker by the jersey. He dragged him over to Perry McDougal. Perry would be filling in at tailback for the first time. "Parker, you're going to have to help Perry," said Mitch. "Whenever we're off the field, you guys stick together like glue. Keep going over the plays with him — and the changes in signals. Okay?"

"Sure," answered Parker. "Good idea."

As the two teams took to the field, Coach Isaac called Parker over to his side.

"Parker, I want you to keep your eyes open," he said. "Maybe you'll be able to give us a different perspective on what's happening on the field. Could be useful. Let me know if you come up with anything."

The coach was asking him to help! That meant he trusted Parker.

A few scattered snowflakes had started to fall. Parker didn't even notice them. Even though he was benched, he still felt like part of the team. And the coach was counting on him to help out!

There was no way he could sit on the bench. He knelt down with one knee on the icy ground near the sideline.

The minute the Kudzu offense took over the ball, there wasn't just snow in the air — there was excitement. It was the first chance the Piranhas had to notice the change in the roster.

Mitch gave them their first surprise right off.

As the two teams got ready on the Kudzus' twenty-five yard line, Parker studied the Piranha defense. They'll probably count on a typical running play, he thought. Still, they appeared ready to move in on the quarterback if it looked like he was going to pass.

What was going through Mitch's mind? he wondered. Where would he put the ball? On the ground or in the air?

Parker could hear Mitch call the switched signal.

"Nineteen! Eleven! Seven! Hike!"

The replacement quarterback skipped back two steps — and then lunged forward! He never gave up the ball. Instead, he carried it himself through a hole opened up by Tru Ballinger and Morris Comer.

Racing by the surprised defensive line, Mitch made his way across the midfield stripe. He was brought down by a Piranha safety who just managed to outrace him.

Watching from the sideline, Parker could see the confusion in the Piranhas' defense. Their captain gathered them in a huddle. It looked as though they were arguing.

Whoever bought our plays from Spike is probably getting some flack, he thought. I wonder who it was — and if they all paid him to get the plays from Spike? They'll probably never trust him again.

Trust, yeah, that's what's important, he thought.

Another thought burrowed deeper in his mind: the only way to gain someone's trust is to tell the truth. Always. Not just once in a while. Not just "shaving the edge off." No fibs or white lies. Just the plain old truth.

A loud cheer from the stands brought his attention back to the field.

The Kudzus had brought the ball down to within scoring distance. A series of running plays kept the ball safely in their own hands.

But by this time, the Piranhas' defense had wised up. They couldn't depend on inside info anymore. Instead, they just played the best they could. Since they hadn't used up much of their energy yet, they had plenty of stamina left. Enough to keep the Kudzus from simply coasting into the end zone.

The next two plays went nowhere, and Mitch called a time out.

Parker had been watching the game carefully — and thought he noticed something. When Mitch came over to the sideline to talk to Coach Isaac, Parker joined them.

"Their nose tackle is reading my mind," Mitch complained. "Even with the changed signals, they've been in on the last two plays."

"You're telling them with your head," Parker piped up. "Remember what Terry noticed about the Leopards' quarterback? If it's a pass or a run to one side, you turn in that direction when you come out of the huddle. It's a dead giveaway."

"Right," said Coach Isaac. "And then the nose tackle shifts a little to that side when you line up. The rest of the defense takes their signals from him."

"Wow! I'll just look straight ahead from now on," said Mitch. "Thanks a lot!"

He ran off to the Kudzus' huddle.

"Nice spotting," said Coach Isaac. "Could make a big difference."

It did.

On the next play, Mitch looked straight ahead when they broke from the huddle.

The Piranhas shuffled around as they lined up. Confused and overeager, they made a mistake. Before Mitch finished calling signals, a whistle blew.

Offside: Piranhas.

The penalty was half the distance to the goal.

"If Perry could get behind Mitch, he could almost hoist him over," joked Rook.

"That's just about what they'll look for," said Parker. "Another quarterback sneak. I'd stick with the screen pass to Moose."

"Let's see if that's what Mitch has in mind," said the coach.

It was.

Moose snagged the ball standing up for another Kudzu touchdown.

"I guess we're all on the same track." Coach Isaac smiled. He looked over at Parker and added, "You'd better get that brain of yours working in your math class. I need my number-one tailback out there."

Parker couldn't remember anyone saying anything like that to him in a long time. Not since his dad had died.

After making the extra point, the Kudzu offense came off the field.

Mitch was all smiles. Perry looked pretty happy, too. He had made a couple of good runs.

"Looks like I'm going to have my work cut out to keep my slot," said Parker.

"Naw, Park," said Cris. "We miss you in the huddle. Nobody tells us any stories anymore."

Parker tried to snap a damp towel at the wise-guy receiver. Instead it crunched, frozen in the cold.

The guys all laughed as Cris gave Parker a friendly punch on the arm.

The Piranha offense wasn't giving up on the field. Their quarterback was calling a terrific game. Between short quick passes and running plays, he gave the Kudzu defense something to think about. .

Parker looked at the clock on the scoreboard. There was less than a minute to play.

The Piranhas had the ball on the Kudzu thirty-two yard line. It was their third down.

With his blockers holding off the Kudzu defense, the Piranhas quarterback drew way back, positioned himself, and hurled a long pass to his wide receiver deep in the end zone.

It was a perfect spiral, aimed right at his target.

But Damien Roberts, the Kudzu safety, was all ready for it. He swooped by the surprised Piranha receiver and grabbed the ball in midair.

Then he took off down the field. He was knocked offside by the tailback Lee Wasser, the only Piranha within range.

The Kudzu offense took over with seconds left and let the clock run out. When the final whistle blew, the score stood Kudzus 21–Piranhas 7.

There was so much cheering and excitement in the locker room, Parker thought he'd never be able to get dressed and leave. Every time he turned around, someone would pour soda pop all over him — as if it were the Super Bowl or something!

But finally he managed to shower and escape along with Mitch, Cris, and Huey.

"That was some game," said Joni, catching up with them. "But what happened during the half? Did you try the envelope? Did it —"

She was interrupted by the arrival of Melissa.

"Parker, what's wrong?" asked the shivering fifth grader. "Aren't you freezing? You didn't even play the second half! Did you break something?"

"Oh, boy." Cris laughed. "Here come's a good one. Go ahead Parker, tell her how it was."

"Yeah," added Huey. "I can't wait to hear the Parker Nolan version."

"What are you guys talking about?" asked Joni.

"Hold your horses, everyone," said Parker. "There is only one story, and that's the one I'm going to tell. You see, I did break something."

"You did?" they all asked at the same time.

"Yep," he admitted. "I broke something real bad. I broke my . . . my pattern."

"Your running pattern? Or your storytelling pattern?" asked Joni.

"You can be sure it wasn't my running pattern," he said.

"What, no more lies?" cried Melissa.

"I don't know what else I can say." Parker smiled. "Except I'm freezing. Let's go get some hot chocolate. I'll treat."

"You heard him," shouted Huey.

"I'm a witness," agreed Cris.

"Hey, Melissa, do you have any money?" asked Parker in a loud whisper. "I'm broke."

Melissa looked over at Joni, who burst out laughing.

Parker was standing behind his sister. In his hand, he was waving a five-dollar bill.